Karen's Chicken Pox

**Other books by
Ann M. Martin**

P. S. Longer Letter Later
(written with Paula Danziger)
Leo the Magnificat
Rachel Parker, Kindergarten Show-off
Eleven Kids, One Summer
Ma and Pa Dracula
Yours Turly, Shirley
Ten Kids, No Pets
With You and Without You
Me and Katie (the Pest)
Stage Fright
Inside Out
Bummer Summer

For older readers:

Missing Since Monday
Just a Summer Romance
Slam Book

THE BABY-SITTERS CLUB series
THE BABY-SITTERS CLUB mysteries
THE KIDS IN MS. COLMAN'S CLASS series
BABY-SITTERS LITTLE SISTER series
(see inside book covers for a complete listing)

Little Sister

Karen's Chicken Pox
Ann M. Martin

Illustrations by Susan Crocca Tang

A
LITTLE APPLE
PAPERBACK

SCHOLASTIC INC.
New York Toronto London Auckland Sydney
Mexico City New Delhi Hong Kong

*The author gratefully acknowledges
Stephanie Calmenson
for her help
with this book.*

ISBN 0-590-52382-1

Copyright © 1999 by Ann M. Martin. Illustrations copyright © 1999 by Scholastic Inc. All rights reserved. Published by Scholastic Inc. THE BABY-SITTERS LITTLE SISTER, LITTLE APPLE PAPERBACKS, and associated logos are trademarks and/or registered trademarks of Scholastic Inc.

12 11 10 9 8 7 6 5 4 3 2 1   9/9 0 1 2 3 4/0

Printed in the U.S.A.   40
First Scholastic printing, October 1999

1

The Perfect Pumpkin

"Hey! You bumped my arm," I said.

"Sorry," Natalie replied.

I was sitting at my school desk drawing pumpkin faces. Natalie Springer sits next to me. She was bending down to pull up her socks when she bumped my chair. (Her socks droop a lot.)

I looked at the pumpkin face I had been working on. Thanks to being bumped, my pumpkin now had a big, jagged line down his cheek. He looked very spooky.

I needed to draw a really excellent pumpkin. I will tell you why. But first I should tell you who I am. My name is Karen Brewer. I am seven years old. I have blonde hair, blue eyes, and a bunch of freckles. I am a glasses-wearer. I even have two pairs. The blue pair is for reading. The pink pair is for the rest of the time.

I am in the second grade at Stoneybrook Academy. My two best friends are in my class. They are Hannie Papadakis and Nancy Dawes. We all used to sit together at the back of the room. But I had to move up front when I got my glasses because my teacher, Ms. Colman, said I could see better there. Now we all wave to one another a lot.

Ms. Colman is the best teacher, by the way. We always do interesting things in her class. And she hardly ever raises her voice. (Sometimes she has to remind me not to raise *my* voice. I get excited in class and call out. That is when Ms. Colman says, "Indoor voice, please, Karen.")

Anyway, the reason I was drawing

pumpkin faces was that Ms. Colman had brought our class a pumpkin to carve and keep in our room for Halloween, which was just a few weeks away. We would each put one favorite drawing into a witch's hat. Then Ms. Colman would pick a drawing out of the hat and carve our class pumpkin to look just like it. So I needed an excellent pumpkin in case mine got picked.

"Hey, Karen, how many pumpkins are you drawing?" asked Ricky.

Ricky Torres sits on the other side of me. (He is my pretend husband. We got married on the playground at recess one day.)

He had three pumpkins. I counted mine.

"Seven," I said. "I want to make sure I have plenty to choose from."

"Class, you have just a few minutes left to work," said Ms. Colman.

Uh-oh. I quickly finished the face I was working on. Then I spread out all my drawings. I had friendly faces, silly faces, and spooky faces. It was time to choose one.

There was no contest. The beady-eyed, pointy-nosed pumpkin with seven snaggly teeth, crooked eyebrows, and the big, jagged line running down his cheek was perfect.

"Thanks, Natalie," I said. "Your bump gave me the perfect pumpkin."

2

Karen's Stories

"Hi, Karen. How was school?" asked Nannie.

"Karen home!" said Emily. She held out her arms to give me a hug.

Nannie is my stepgrandmother. She was holding my little sister, Emily Michelle, on her hip. (Emily is two and a half.) I had just walked into the house after school, and they were happy to see me.

For the month of October I was living at my big house. Last month I lived at my little house. That is right. I have two houses. I will tell you how that happened.

The story starts when I was very little. Back then I lived only in the big house here in Stoneybrook, Connecticut. I lived with Mommy, Daddy, and Andrew. (Andrew is my little brother. He is four going on five.)

Then Mommy and Daddy started having troubles. They argued a lot. It was awful. They tried their best to work things out, but just could not do it. So they explained to Andrew and me that though they love each of us very much, they could not live together anymore. Then they got divorced.

Mommy moved with Andrew and me to a little house not far away in Stoneybrook. She met a very nice man named Seth. She and Seth got married, which means that Seth is my stepfather.

Daddy stayed in the big house after the divorce. (It is the house he grew up in.) He met a very nice woman named Elizabeth, and they got married. Elizabeth was married once before and has four children. They are David Michael, who is seven, like me; Kristy, who is thirteen and the best stepsister ever; and Sam and Charlie, who are so old they are in high school. When Daddy and Elizabeth married, Kristy, David Michael, Sam, and Charlie became my stepsister and stepbrothers.

Emily joined the family a little later. Daddy and Elizabeth adopted her from a faraway country called Vietnam. That is when Nannie came to live with us. Nannie is Elizabeth's mother. She came to help out with Emily, but she really helps everyone.

Now Andrew and I switch houses almost every month — a month at the big house, a month at the little house. Back and forth. That way we get to spend time with each of our two families. That is a good thing because I love both my families.

Also, there are pets at both houses. Emily Junior, my pet rat (I named her after Emily, of course), and Bob, Andrew's hermit crab, go back and forth with Andrew and me. At the little house are Midgie, Seth's dog, and Rocky, Seth's cat. The pets at the big house are Shannon, David Michael's big Bernese mountain dog puppy; Pumpkin, our new black kitten; Crystal Light the Second, my goldfish; and Goldfishie, Andrew's hedgehog. (Just kidding! He's a fish.)

Andrew and I have two of lots of our things because it makes going back and forth between our houses easier. We each have two sets of toys and clothes and books. I have two stuffed cats. (Goosie lives at the little house. Moosie lives at the big house.) We each have two bicycles. (I taught Andrew to ride a two-wheeler!) And you know about my two best friends, Hannie and Nancy. Hannie lives across the street and one house over from the big house. Nancy lives next door to the little house. We call ourselves the Three Musketeers because we like to do everything together.

Because Andrew and I have two of so many things, I call us Andrew Two-Two and Karen Two-Two. I thought up those names after my teacher, Ms. Colman, read a book to our class. It was called *Jacob Two-Two Meets the Hooded Fang*.

So that is the story of my houses. Now it was time to tell another story. Nannie and Emily wanted to hear the story of my day. So over cookies and milk in the kitchen, I told them.

I Will Be Right Back!

Halloween was coming closer and my friends and I still had not decided what costumes we would wear. At recess one day we had a serious talk.

"Clowns! We should be three circus clowns," said Hannie.

"I do not know about clowns," said Nancy. "But we should be three of something."

"We could go as the real Three Musketeers," I said.

"Or the Three Blind Mice," said Nancy.

"Maybe we should be three things that go together but are not the same," I said.

"Good idea," said Hannie. "We can be three animals. We can be jungle animals."

"Or farm animals," said Nancy.

Ringgg! The bell rang, ending recess.

"To be continued," I said.

Hannie and I continued our conversation on the school bus that afternoon.

We promised to call Nancy if we had any bright ideas.

"We could be vehicles," I said. "I could be a school bus."

"I could be an airplane," said Hannie.

"I will call Nancy when I get home to see what she would want to be," I said.

By the time we got off the bus, we had several good ideas. I ran into the house to call Nancy. But Sam was on the phone. (Lately he had been on the phone a lot.)

"I will be right back!" I called to whomever else was at home.

"Where are you going? You just walked

in," said Daddy, coming out of his office. (Daddy works at home most days.)

"Sam is on the phone and I want to call Nancy," I said. "I am going to Hannie's house."

"Cross carefully, please," said Daddy. "And come right back after your phone call."

"I always cross carefully. And I promise to come right back," I said.

I ran out of the house. I really do always cross carefully. I stopped at the curb and looked both ways before I walked across the street. Then I ran up Hannie's walk and rang her bell.

"Sam is on the phone. We need to call Nancy from here," I said when she opened the door.

We told Nancy our ideas. She had three more of her own. I ran back home.

"Are you ready for a snack?" asked Nannie.

"Yes, thank you. I am really hungry," I said.

That gave me another idea. I wanted to call Hannie and Nancy and tell it to them. But Sam was still on the phone.

"I will be right back!" I said.

"Where are you going?" asked Nannie.

I explained about the phone calls.

"Your snack will be waiting. Don't stay long," said Nannie.

I went back outside, stopped at the curb, looked both ways, crossed the street, rang the bell, told Hannie my ideas, called Nancy, and came back home.

A plate of peanut butter on crackers and a glass of apple juice were waiting for me. When I finished my snack, Sam was still on the phone. I hoped Hannie and Nancy were not trying to call me.

"I will be right back!" I said.

I ran to Hannie's house again to see if she had any new ideas. She was on the phone with Nancy. They both had more ideas for our costumes. By the time I had to leave to start my homework, we had a long list.

4

Making Plans

"It is time to vote," I said.

It was Thursday. I was on the playground at recess again with my friends. It was time to decide what we were going to be for Halloween. We had narrowed our list down to two choices: farm animals or wacky vegetables. We agreed to vote by making sounds. Animal noises, or crunches and squishes. (Some vegetables are crunchy and others are squishy.)

"I will count to three," said Nancy. "One, two, three!"

16

We answered at the same time.

"Cluck!"

"Moo!"

"Baa!"

We started giggling.

(Pamela Harding and her friends, Jannie Gilbert and Leslie Morris, gave us meanie-mo faces. Pamela is my best enemy. She likes to make fun of me every chance she gets.)

"I am not surprised we all want to be animals," I said.

"I am glad we each picked a different animal," said Hannie.

Hannie was going to be a cow. Nancy was going to be a sheep. I wanted to be a chicken. *Cluck!*

"A grown-up is going to have to come trick-or-treating with us," I said. "I think whoever comes should wear overalls."

"Like Old MacDonald!" said Nancy.

Back in our classroom we had more Halloween planning to do. Ms. Colman said we could have a class party.

"I am going to pass around a sign-up sheet," said Ms. Colman. "Please write down what you will be able to bring to the party."

I wrote down two things. One was "witches' brew." That was soda or juice. The other was "bat cakes." That was chocolate cupcakes. They are one of Nannie's specialties.

Did I tell you that Nannie has her very own candy-making business? She works at home in the second kitchen, which used to be a pantry. I am her very good assistant. I even helped her win the Cocoa-Best cooking contest once. So "witches' brew" and "bat cakes" would be easy.

"Our party will be on the Friday before Halloween. That is a week from tomorrow," said Ms. Colman.

This was so cool. A party at school and Halloween on Sunday. Halloween on a weekend is the best. There is plenty of time to have fun!

Baby-sitting for Emily

I was still in a great mood by the time I got home. I burst through the door.

"Hi, everyone!" I called.

"Hi, Karen," said Andrew.

I heard another voice say "Hi." It was David Michael's. I followed his voice to the kitchen. Nannie and Emily were there too.

"Did you have a good day?" asked Nannie.

"I did," I replied. "I will need your help making bat cakes. They are chocolate cupcakes."

I told everyone about my Halloween plans.

"I will be happy to help out," said Nannie. "Can you help me out this afternoon? Emily is not feeling very well. She has a little bit of fever, and her head hurts. I need you to look after her while I am cooking dinner."

I had noticed that Nannie had not put Emily down since I walked in. Emily was resting her head on Nannie's shoulder. I patted Emily on the back.

"I will take care of you," I said.

Bringgg! Nannie answered the phone. It was Elizabeth. She was asking about Emily.

"I do not think we need to take her to the doctor yet," said Nannie. "I think she just has a little cold."

When I finished eating my snack, I took Emily into the den. Andrew came with us and watched cartoons for awhile. Then he went upstairs to look for Pumpkin.

I turned off the TV.

"Do you want to sing some songs, Emily?" I asked.

"Karen sing to Emily," Emily said.

First I sang "Bingo the Dog." After "Bingo" I sang "Where Is Thumbkin?" I helped Emily wiggle all the right fingers. Then I sang "Old MacDonald." That made me think of my Halloween costume.

"I am going to sing the song again," I said. "Listen carefully and guess what animal I am going to be on Halloween."

Emily guessed every animal in the song.

"I am going to be only one animal. I am going to be a chicken," I said. "What do you want to be for Halloween?"

Emily said something that sounded like "gote."

"What was that?" I asked her.

"Gote," said Emily loudly.

"Oh, a *ghost*. That is a good idea. I can help you make your costume. Would you like that?" I asked.

"Karen help Emmie," said Emily.

"That is right. I will help you. I promise," I said.

6

Karen's Good Idea

Nannie made one of my favorite dinners. Spaghetti with meatballs and a salad.

While we were eating, I told the rest of my family my Halloween news. I was not the only one with interesting news. Sam had some too. (Sam usually manages to stay off the phone at dinnertime. That is because he likes to eat.) Did I tell you that Sam is president of his class? Well, he is. That means he has important jobs to do all the time.

"I am organizing a fund-raiser for Halloween weekend," said Sam. "But that is

Homecoming weekend. There is going to be a football game and a dance. Practically everyone I have asked to help me has said they will be too busy. And if we do not raise money, we will have to cancel our class trip this spring."

"What kind of fund-raiser are you planning?" asked Elizabeth.

"I wanted to hold a bake sale. Those usually do well," said Sam. "I figured if just a handful of kids at school baked some things, we would be all right. But I cannot find even a handful to help."

Hmm. I had an idea. I decided it was my day for helping my family.

"Does it matter who does the baking for the sale?" I asked.

"No, just as long as the food is good and we have enough," said Sam.

"I am in charge of making bat cakes for my class. Those are cupcakes, in case you did not know. We could make cupcakes for you too," I said. "If the whole family helped, we could make lots of things!"

"I will do some baking," said Kristy.

"Me too," said Charlie. "I already promised to help with the selling. But I will help with the baking too."

"Thanks a lot, Karen," said Sam. "I did not think about asking you guys, but why not? We have some of the best bakers in town right here at this table."

The phone rang, and Sam jumped up to answer it.

The next thing we knew, *crash*! Emily knocked her cup of milk to the floor. She started to cry.

"That is all right," said Daddy. "We can get you more milk."

Elizabeth picked up Emily to soothe her, but she was crying hard and would not stop.

"Poor baby," said Elizabeth. She touched her lips to Emily's forehead. "She definitely has a fever."

Daddy brought a fresh cup of milk. But Emily did not want it. It seemed that all she wanted to do was cry.

7

Emily's Itchies

On Friday after school, Nancy's mother picked up the Three Musketeers. We were going to the crafts store downtown to buy what we needed for our costumes.

First we stopped at the Rosebud Cafe for a snack. I had waffles with strawberries. (I am glad I am not really a chicken. They do not get to eat snacks like that!)

We talked about what we would each need to buy.

"I am going to be a black-and-white cow,"

26

said Hannie. "I will wear white clothes and iron black patches on them."

"You should get a bell to wear around your neck," I said.

"Good idea! Thanks," said Hannie.

Nancy said she wanted to be a party sheep.

"I am going to wear colored ribbons. That will make my costume more fun," she said.

"All I need is a bag of yellow feathers," I said. "I will glue them on my big yellow sweatshirt."

"What are you going to wear on your legs?" asked Hannie.

"I am not sure yet. I was thinking of wearing orange leggings. Do you think that would make me look like a chicken?"

"Sounds good," said Nancy.

"You girls are going to look wonderful," said Mrs. Dawes. "Come, we should get going."

We headed for the crafts store. We found everything we needed.

That night we had a quiet dinner at home. Kristy was out baby-sitting. Sam and Charlie had gone to an early movie. Emily was still feeling sick.

When we finished eating, I watched *The Addams Family* with David Michael, Andrew, and Emily. I can watch *The Addams Family* any time of year. But they are definitely best at Halloween. I like to make believe I am Wednesday Addams. I cross my arms, snap my fingers, and sing the theme song. I love the part about how "they're creepy and they're kooky, mysterious and spooky." I know the whole song by heart.

While we were watching, I noticed that Emily could not sit still. First I thought she was bored. I do not know how anyone could be bored with *The Addams Family*. But I decided maybe a two-and-a-half-year-old could get bored.

Then I noticed that Emily was not just squirming. She was scratching herself.

"Are you a little monkey?" I asked.

Emily looked as if she were going to cry.

Squirm. Scratch. Squirm. Scratch. It seemed to get worse during all my favorite parts. I was having trouble paying attention. But I did not want to say anything. I knew if I did she would start to cry. Then I would miss the whole show.

Watching the show with Emily was not much fun. I was glad when Elizabeth decided to take her to the doctor the next day. It was time to find out what was wrong with Emily.

8

An Important Job

On Saturday Elizabeth took Emily to the doctor early in the morning. It was a good thing too. Emily woke up feeling worse than she had the night before.

Everyone else was awake and at the breakfast table by the time I got up.

"Charlie and I are going to the supermarket to buy baking supplies. Does anyone need anything?" asked Sam.

"We could use some juice," said Nannie.

"Pretzels, please!" said Andrew.

"No problem. We will pick some up," said Charlie.

"Can I go shopping with you?" I asked.

A ride in the Junk Bucket with my two big brothers sounded like fun. (The Junk Bucket is what we call Charlie's rattly old car.)

"Sure. The family baking project was your idea. You are welcome to help out any way you like," said Sam.

Sam had to make a few calls after breakfast. (I am sure you are not surprised.) Then we headed out.

The first thing we did was pick up the pretzels and the juice so we would not forget them. While we were near the dairy section, I reminded my brothers that we would need plenty of eggs for baking.

"Thanks, Karen," said Charlie.

"Of course Karen knows all about eggs," said Sam. "She is going to be a chicken for Halloween."

"Cluck, cluck!" I replied.

We also picked up some butter. Then we found the aisle with the baking supplies.

Sam and Charlie put flour, sugar, baking powder, and baking soda into the shopping cart.

"That should do it," said Sam.

"Hold it!" I said. "We are not done. If your cupcakes look special, they will sell better."

I found coconut flakes, sprinkles, black and white chocolate chips, and cans of colored frosting.

"Karen, what would we do without you!" said Sam.

"You would have a very boring bake sale," I replied.

"You are right. The bake sale needs you. In fact, how would you like to work for awhile at the sale table?" asked Charlie.

"Really?" I said. "I mean, of course! You need my help, and I will be there."

I was so excited. My big brothers hardly ever needed my help. But now they really did. And this was an important job.

"Before we go, is there anything here you could use for your costume?" asked Charlie.

"I do not think so," I replied.

"How about chicken feed? You could carry a little bag with some grain in it," said Sam.

"That would be fun," I replied. "Thanks."

We got a box of cornmeal and some baggies. Then we went to the checkout counter. A display of colored bandannas was near the magazine rack.

"How about a bandanna to wear around your neck? You will be the best-dressed chicken in Stoneybrook," said Sam.

It took awhile for me to pick a color. Red, green, yellow, pink, blue. I ended up choosing a red one.

I was having so much fun! I was going to help Sam raise all the money his class needed for their spring trip. I was going to have the best costume. And it was going to be the best Halloween ever.

9

Emily's Chicken Pox

"We are home!" I called.

Sam, Charlie, and I walked into the house carrying our armloads of grocery bags. We were laughing and talking.

Daddy, Elizabeth, and Nannie were in the kitchen talking. They looked serious.

"Is anything wrong?" asked Charlie.

"Emily and I went to see the doctor. It turns out that she has more than a cold. She has chicken pox," Elizabeth replied.

"Wow! How could she get chicken pox? She had a shot just like I did, right?" I asked.

"Yes, she did," replied Daddy. "But it is still possible to get chicken pox. Thanks to the shot, we expect it to be a mild case."

"Does she have spots? I did not see any," I said. "Maybe the doctor made a mistake."

"I saw spots on her belly when I was dressing her this morning," replied Elizabeth.

"No wonder she was scratching so much last night. Poor Emily," I said.

"We have already spoken with David Michael, Andrew, and Kristy about what this means for our family over the next week or so. They have had the chicken pox, so they know all about it," said Daddy. "While you are unpacking your groceries, we will talk with the three of you."

Boo. I felt bad for Emily. I really did. But I felt a little bad for me too. I had been having so much fun. Now everyone was gigundoly serious.

I listened to Elizabeth say that she could use our help.

"For the next few days, Emily will need to

be kept quiet and cool. And we all have to to make sure she does not scratch her pox. If she does, she could end up with scars," said Elizabeth.

Uh-oh. I should have told Emily to stop scratching last night. I hoped she would be okay.

"Emily will also have to be quarantined for a few days," said Daddy. "That means being kept apart from other people."

"I am sorry to say it means no friends in the house," said Elizabeth. "Just for awhile."

I gave a little sigh. But I was not too upset. The Three Musketeers could always go to Hannie's or Nancy's house.

Elizabeth thought of a few more things we would need to do. While she was talking, I was thinking. I was thinking that Emily had had the shot, but she still got chicken pox. I had had the shot too, and I had thought I could not get them. Now I was not so sure.

"Um, excuse me," I said. "If a person had the shot, how catching are the chicken pox?"

"I do not know," said Elizabeth. "We know that they are very catching without the shot. That is the reason for the quarantine. We do not want to take the chance of exposing anyone who is not protected."

Hmm. Halloween was getting closer. I had had the shot, but I still did not want to take any chances. I needed a good plan for protecting myself. I thought of one fast.

It did not seem like a good time to tell everyone my plan. I decided I would talk to Daddy in private later.

10

Karen's Worries

Knock, knock. After lunch I knocked on Daddy's office door. Even though it was Saturday, he was working. I did not like to disturb him, but I had important things on my mind.

"Can I talk to you a minute?" I asked.

"Of course. Come in," replied Daddy.

"It is about Emily," I said.

"What about Emily?"

"I am afraid of catching her chicken pox," I said. "It is almost Halloween. I have a lot to do."

"I am sorry it's so close to Halloween. But the chances of your getting sick are very small," said Daddy.

"I am still worried. So I think I should go live somewhere else until Emily is better," I said. "I love my little sister. But I cannot take any chances with getting sick."

"Karen, I do not want you living somewhere else. We would all miss you too much. Especially Emily. If you are here, you can help her," said Daddy.

"I already promised to help Hannie and Nancy make their costumes. If I get sick, I cannot do that. They would be very sad without me. And what about Sam? He needs me too. I promised to help with his bake sale," I said. "I cannot help him if I get sick."

I did not want to sound like a selfish meanie-mo, so I did not tell Daddy that I would be very upset if I missed dressing up as a chicken and trick-or-treating with my friends because I was sick.

Ooh! Maybe I should have picked a different farm animal to be for Halloween. Maybe it was not a good idea to be a *chicken* when my sister had *chicken* pox! I thought for a minute about changing to another animal. But I really wanted to be a chicken. I already had what I needed for my costume. And I knew it would not make any difference.

"Karen, I understand what you are saying. If you get sick, it could ruin all your plans. But you have already been exposed. Moving out is not going to help now," Daddy replied. "I am sorry."

Boo, bullfrogs . . . and chicken pox!

11

Staying Away

My talk with Daddy had not gone the way I wanted it to. It was true that I had already been exposed. But that did not mean I had to be exposed even more.

I stomped upstairs to my room and shut the door. Maybe I could not move out. But I was going to stay as far away from Emily as possible.

I knew it would be hard. She would be eating at the same table. She would be sleeping in a room near mine. She would be breathing the same air! I tried holding my breath. But I could not do it for very long. Finally I had to give in and breathe. I gasped so hard I probably took in twice as many germs.

I thought about calling Hannie and Nancy and going to one of their houses for the rest of the day. But I knew they had plans with their families. It was raining hard, so I stayed in my room most of the afternoon. I finished my homework and read whatever books were lying around.

Nannie and Elizabeth each came to my room to ask if I would help out with Emily. They wanted me to read her a story or play a game with her.

"I have to stay here until my homework is done. It is an extra-important assignment," I said.

I left my room only twice. One time I went to the bathroom, and the other time I got a snack. Each time I made sure Emily was not around.

At dinner, I raced for a seat at the other end of the table from Emily. (I almost knocked David Michael over trying to get to it.)

I watched Daddy try to keep Emily from scratching. Every time she started, he would take her hands in his and play a finger game.

"Where is Thumbkin? Where is Thumbkin?" he sang.

Ugh. I did not want to get itchies like Emily.

"How is your homework assignment coming along, Karen?" asked Elizabeth.

"It is a very long assignment. I am still working on it," I replied.

"What is it about?" asked Nannie.

"Um, it is about . . . Nannie, you do not want to know. It would take me too long to explain it," I replied.

"Maybe you need to take a break from your homework tonight," said Elizabeth. "If you have trouble finishing it, you can explain to Ms. Colman that you had to help your sister. I am sure she would understand."

"Emily was asking for you all afternoon. Right, Emmie?" said Kristy.

"Karen play?" said Emily.

"You could read Emily her bedtime story," said Kristy. "She would like that."

"I am not in the mood to read any stories," I replied.

"Come on. We have to help keep Emily's mind off of the itchies. You and I can read to her together," said Kristy.

"All right. If I am not too busy later, I will help you," I said.

I was going to make sure I was busy. Even if it meant cleaning up my room!

That is exactly what I did. I cleaned. When Daddy came in to ask if I would help bathe Emily, I was under my bed clearing out all the socks and things that were hiding there.

"I am sorry. I am too busy now," I said.

When Kristy came in, I was straightening out my closet.

"Sorry," I said. "I have been meaning to do this for ages."

My family was getting annoyed. But I did not care. I was annoyed too. I was annoyed that nobody cared if I caught the chicken pox and missed Halloween.

12

"Abracadabra!"

On Monday at school, Hannie and Nancy asked how I was feeling.

"Fine," I replied. "Thank goodness."

I had told my friends the sad story of Emily and the chicken pox when I saw them on Sunday. (We played at Hannie's house. That got me out of the big house for awhile, which was a good thing.)

I made my friends promise not to tell anyone that my sister had chicken pox. What if I got it? Everyone would think I was weird. Chicken pox is a baby disease.

48

"Do not worry," said Nancy. "I thought of a plan last night. Since it is almost Halloween, all you have to do is say a magic spell to keep from getting sick."

I looked over my shoulder to make sure no one was listening. We were in the back of our classroom waiting for Ms. Colman to arrive. No one seemed to be paying any attention to us. But I was not taking any chances.

"Whisper the spell to me," I said.

"Abracadabra, pix, pax, pox. Stay away, germs. And stay away, spots!" said Nancy.

"When do I say it?" I asked.

"You say it three times a day. Once when you wake up, once at recess, and once at bedtime," said Nancy.

"Thanks," I replied. "It is worth trying."

"I had an idea too," said Hannie.

This was good. I needed all the help I could get.

Just then Ms. Colman arrived.

"Good morning, class. Please take your seats," she said.

"Tell me your idea at recess," I said to Hannie.

I could hardly wait. If I followed Nancy's instructions *and* Hannie's, I was sure I would not get sick.

Hannie told us her idea as soon as we were on the playground.

"You have to eat lots of grapefruit with lemon juice," said Hannie.

Ugh. I puckered my mouth. "Why?"

"I think I read somewhere that sour stuff kills germs. You would kill every germ in the world if you ate grapefruit with lemon juice," said Hannie.

"Can I put sugar on it?" I asked.

"No, you cannot! It would ruin the power."

"Okay. I will do it," I said. "I will do anything not to get sick!"

I was glad we had a library period in the afternoon. It gave me a chance to do some research. I read that it can take a couple of weeks after being exposed to chicken pox germs before you get sick.

50

That was interesting. But I did not know when I had first been exposed to Emily's germs. Maybe it was just in time for me to get sick on Halloween.

I decided to say Nancy's magic spell then and there. I did not want to wait for bedtime. I said it to myself so no one would hear.

"Abracadabra, pix, pax, pox. Stay away, germs. And stay away, spots!"

At home, I ate a grapefruit with lemon juice before dinner. (I did not let anyone see me add the lemon juice.)

And I kept away from Emily. That was the hardest thing to do.

"Karen, I wish you would spend more time with your sister," said Daddy. "We all have to pitch in and help."

"All right, I promise," I said.

I promised to help my sister. I just did not say *which* sister.

13

Just a Little Cold

The first thing I did when I woke up on Tuesday was say Nancy's spell. At least I tried to. I was having trouble remembering the words.

"Abracadabra, pox, pax, pix. Stay away, germs. Pick up sticks?"

No. That was not it. I could not think straight. I could not see straight either. My eyes hurt. My whole body hurt.

I made myself get out of bed and look in the mirror. No spots, thank goodness.

A few kids in my class had colds. I had

probably caught one of theirs. A couple more days of saying the spell and eating grapefruit with lemon would cure me for sure. That was all I needed.

I tried hard to remember the spell. It came back to me after a few tries. I felt better the minute I said it. I got dressed and went downstairs.

Nannie had a grapefruit ready for me.

"I never knew you liked grapefruit so much, Karen. I am glad," said Nannie.

When no one was looking, I poured some lemon juice on it. I ate it fast so I would not taste it too much.

"Karen help Emmie?" said Emily.

I smiled at my little sister. I knew she wanted me to make her costume. With just a few days left until Halloween, it was probably safe for me to be around her again.

"I will help you soon," I replied.

I ate a muffin with jelly to wipe out the sour taste in my mouth. Then I got my jacket. And a scarf. And a hat. And gloves. I was feeling a little chilly.

When I arrived at the bus stop, Hannie was waiting for me.

"Hi! I have been following your instructions," I said.

"That is good. I am sure you will be okay for Halloween," said Hannie.

I did not tell her that I was shivering inside my jacket. That was the bad news. The good news was that Hannie did not say anything about suddenly seeing spots on me.

At school, I forgot all about my shivers. I had a very good reason. Before lunch, Ms. Colman picked a pumpkin design out of the witch's hat. Guess whose design she picked? Mine!

"Congratulations, Karen," said Ms. Colman. "You drew a wonderful, spooky pumpkin for our classroom."

I got to scoop out pumpkin seeds and oversee the carving so the pumpkin looked just like my drawing.

Beady eyes. Pointy nose. Seven snaggly

teeth. Crooked eyebrows. And a big jagged line running down his cheek.

We talked about our party on Friday. When I told my class that Nannie would be helping with the bat cakes, everyone cheered. (They have tasted Nannie's chocolates before.)

Even if I did not feel so great, I had a very good time at school.

At home, I worked on my costume. I even found a sheet for Emily's ghost costume. Everything was a little harder to do because I did not feel so well. But I was not going to let a little cold stop me.

Just a few more days to go. I was going to be okay.

Spots!

When I woke up on Wednesday, I felt worse than the day before. I thought my little cold must have turned into a big one. Then I looked in the mirror.

"Moosie, help!" I said to my stuffed cat. "I have spots!"

I jumped back into bed and pulled the covers over my head. I had to think of a plan. Maybe I could cover the spots with makeup. Elizabeth kept some in the bathroom. All I had to do was get in there without being seen.

I went to my door and peeked out. The coast was clear. I started to tiptoe to the bathroom. Just then Andrew stepped out of his room.

"Hi, Karen!" he said. "Ooh, you have spots!"

He said it loudly enough for anyone who was upstairs to hear. The next thing I knew I was surrounded by half my family.

"Karen, I am sorry," said Elizabeth. "I know you did not want to get sick now. But you will have to go back to bed."

"But I really do not feel too bad. I can still go to school," I said.

"No, you cannot," said Elizabeth. "Remember the quarantine? You have to be at home for a few days while you are most contagious."

I quickly did some math in my head. I had heard someone say something about five days. Sunday was the fifth day. Sunday was Halloween. I was going to miss Halloween. I was going to miss everything!

I did not say another word. I went back to

my room and climbed into bed. I pulled the covers over my head again. I did not want to see or talk to anyone.

I was going to miss Halloween. And my class party. And helping at Sam's bake sale. I was going to miss my whole life because of a baby disease! It was so humiliating.

Knock, knock.

I peeked out from under the covers. Daddy was standing in my doorway.

"May I come in?" he asked.

I did not want to talk to Daddy. But he was carrying a tray of food. I saw a big glass of juice on it, and I was very thirsty.

"Okay," I replied.

I sat up, and Daddy put the tray on my bed. I took a few gulps of juice.

"I am very sorry this had to happen now," said Daddy.

"It is all Emily's fault," I said.

"She did not mean to make you sick."

"I know. But now *she* can go out on Halloween because she will not be contagious. I have to stay at home," I said.

"I agree, it is terrible."

"I am even mad at Hannie and Nancy. They said they could keep me from getting sick. I said Nancy's magic spell. And I ate all those grapefruits with lemon," I said.

"So that is why you suddenly liked grapefruit. You thought it would keep you from getting sick," said Daddy. "Well, maybe the magic spell and the grapefruit will help you have a milder case of chicken pox."

The minute he said "chicken pox," I started feeling itchy. I had felt a little itchy and squirmy the day before. But I had decided it was only my imagination. Today I was sure my itches were real. I started rubbing my face.

Daddy took my hands in his. "You are too grown-up for 'Where Is Thumbkin?' So how about a two-handed thumb wrestle?"

I tried to smile, but I could not. Today my class was going to make decorations for the party. And here I was sick in bed. And mad at the world.

60

15

Getting Even

"Would you like anything from the store?" asked Nannie.

"No, thank you," I said.

"I will be back soon. I will bring home some soup for lunch. It might help you feel better," said Nannie.

Nannie was going out to buy Halloween decorations for the house. And candy for trick-or-treaters. Now that I was sick, I would not get to be a trick-or-treater.

I was reaching up to scratch an itchy spot when Daddy came in.

"Please try not to scratch," he said. "I will be back with some lotion. That should help you feel better."

Lotion was not going to help. Soup was not going to help. Everyone was trying their best to make me feel better. Kristy had promised to read to me when she got home. Charlie had offered to play games with me. Sam had said I could be his official bake sale consultant. Andrew was going to make me a get-well card. David Michael had told me I could borrow his games and books. Elizabeth was going to make me a special dessert.

But none of it was going to help!

When Daddy returned with the lotion, I told him I did not want it.

"It will make you feel less itchy," said Daddy.

"I do not care. I do not want yucky lotion."

"Karen, I know you are feeling bad. But acting grouchy will not help matters. I will put the lotion on you. Then if you feel well enough to get out of bed, you can help me start decorating the house," said Daddy.

I let Daddy put on the lotion. But I made grouchy faces while he did it.

"Come," said Daddy. "We will see if Emily wants to help us too."

Seeing Emily was the last thing I needed. But getting up and helping sounded a whole lot better than being stuck in bed.

"You two can start putting up spider-webs," said Daddy. "We need them in the corners of the rooms downstairs. I will put up orange streamers. We will have made a good start by the time Nannie comes home with the rest of the decorations."

The three of us went downstairs. When Daddy was not looking, I stuck out my tongue at Emily. She thought it was funny. She did not know I was being a meanie-mo. I decided to try harder. Emily had made me sick, and I wanted to get even.

"Come, Emily," I said. "We need to put spiderwebs in the den."

Emily followed me to the den. I twirled around and dangled a big black rubber spider in front of her.

Emily laughed again. I decided to try even harder.

There was a big bowl of candy corn on the table. I took a handful and popped it into my mouth.

"Yum!" I said.

"Candy!" cried Emily.

"None for Emily. All for me," I said.

I put the bowl way up high where Emily could not reach it. Then I took another handful of candy corn and popped it into my mouth. That did it. Emily started to cry.

Daddy heard and came to see what was wrong. "Karen, what is going on?" he asked.

"Nothing," I replied.

But Emily pointed to the bowl. Daddy knew I had moved it.

"Karen Brewer, I know you are feeling sick. But that is no reason to be unkind," said Daddy.

"Well, it was unkind of Emily to make me sick!" I said. I ran to my room and pulled the covers over my head.

16

Karen Brewer, Germ Queen

In the afternoon, Hannie and Nancy both called me. I asked Daddy to tell them I was too sick to come to the phone.

I knew it was not fair, but I was mad at them too. Their grapefruits and spells had done no good at all. So I did not want to talk to either of them. I did not want to hear how much fun everyone had had getting ready for the class party while I was home sick.

At dinnertime I did not go downstairs. I asked to eat in my room. That way I could stay in bed being mad at everyone and feeling sorry for myself.

Who could blame me? I was missing one thing after another. The next thing I missed was baking with my family for Sam's sale. I could not believe it. It had been my idea to begin with!

But by the time they got started, I was too tired to go downstairs and help. Also, I could not decorate the cupcakes because I was too germy. Karen Brewer, Germ Queen. That was me.

I could hear everyone laughing downstairs.

"Wait! Stop!" said Kristy. "The recipe says a quarter teaspoon of baking powder, not baking soda."

"Oops," said David Michael.

"Let me do it! I know how," said Andrew.

I knew how to do it too. But no one was asking me.

My family tried not to leave me alone upstairs. They took turns coming to visit me. But I was not very friendly.

"You are going to have the first warm cupcake, as soon as it is ready," said Sam. "I will bring you the decorations and you can fix it up the way you like it."

"That is okay," I replied. "You can surprise me."

I did not want to be reminded of how much fun it was to decorate cupcakes when I would be allowed to decorate only one — my own.

When Sam left, Nannie came in.

"I know you are feeling pretty awful. But you promised to help Emily with her costume," she said.

"I am not in the mood anymore," I replied.

My spots were itching. I was trying not to scratch, so I slapped at them instead. It did not help.

"Maybe you will be more in the mood tomorrow," said Nannie.

"I do not think so."

"I wish you would try being nicer to your sister," said Nannie. "But I understand why you are upset. If you do not feel up to help-ing, I will make her costume myself."

"Thank you," I said.

At least Nannie was trying to understand how I felt. It seemed that she was the only one.

17

No Ghost

The next day was Thursday. Only three days until Halloween.

Daddy was in his office. Everyone else had gone to school or work. That left Nannie, Emily, and me. I was lying in bed and could hear Nannie working with Emily on her costume.

"Keep your arms at your sides for a minute," said Nannie. "Good. Do not move."

I pictured Emily standing under the sheet. Nannie must have been marking places to make holes for Emily's eyes, nose, and mouth. She would have to shorten the sheet too, so Emily would not trip.

A little while later, Emily ran down the hallway, past my room. She was wearing her sheet. And she was crying.

"What is wrong?" asked Nannie. "Why is my little ghost unhappy?"

"No gose! No!" shouted Emily.

"But you are a very good ghost," said Nannie.

"No, no! Emily *gote!* "

"I do not understand," said Nannie.

Emily started sobbing. It took awhile, but Nannie calmed her down.

"Try again to tell me what you want," said Nannie.

Through her sniffles, Emily said, "Emmie *gote.*"

Then she started singing "Old MacDonald Had a Farm."

Aha! Nannie still did not understand. But I did. Emily knew my friends and I were going to be farm animals. Now she wanted to be one too. She wanted to be like the big girls.

"Emily? Do you want to be a goat?" I called from my room.

Emily came running.

"Yes! Goat! I *say* goat! Karen help Emmie?" she said.

"Maybe," I replied.

Nannie poked her head in the door.

"Karen, thank you!" she said. "I could not have figured that out without you."

I was proud I had helped Nannie. And I was proud that Emily wanted to be like her big sister. But I was still mad about being sick. And it was all Emily's fault.

Emily was standing by my bed singing "Old MacDonald" again. "WEE-I-E-I-YO!"

She was funny. I could not stay mad at her too long.

"Oh, all right," I said. "I will help you make your costume."

The phone was ringing. Nannie answered it. I heard her say hello to Elizabeth. Eliza-

beth was calling to see how Emily and I were feeling.

The truth was, I was not feeling too bad. My spots were not as itchy.

And now I had a new important job to do. I had to figure out how to make a goat costume for Emily. I had no idea how to do it. But that never stops me from doing something. I always find a way.

18

Apologies All Around

By the afternoon, I still did not have any good ideas for how to make a goat costume. I decided it was time for a little help from my friends. (Now that I was feeling better, I was not mad at them anymore. I knew it was not their fault I got sick.)

I waited until Sam was not hogging the phone, then I grabbed it and called Hannie and Nancy.

"Hi," I said to Hannie. "I am sorry I did not call you back sooner. I was not feeling very good."

"I am sorry you got sick," replied Hannie. "I guess my grapefruit-and-lemon-juice idea was not such a good one."

"That is okay. You did not give me chicken pox," I said. "Anyway, even though I am sick, I have an important job. Maybe you can help me."

I told Hannie about Emily's costume. "She wants to be a farm animal like me. She wants to be a goat. Only I do not know how to make a goat costume."

Hannie had some excellent ideas. I wrote them down. Then I called Nancy. She felt bad that I had gotten sick too.

"I guess my spell did not work out. I am sorry," said Nancy.

"No problem," I said. "It is not your fault."

Nancy had a few more ideas for Emily's costume. I wrote them down next to Hannie's.

Things were shaping up. My friends and I had made apologies all around. And I had some good ideas for Emily's costume.

I knew Nannie would have good ideas too. Pretty soon I had a list of suggestions from my whole family.

Kristy even had a book called *The Book of the Goat*. She let me borrow it. I never knew there were so many different kinds of goats. There are long-haired, short-haired, curly-haired, and straight-haired goats. There are tan ones, black ones, brown ones, white ones, and mixed ones. There are goats with horns, and goats without horns. Wow! I had lots of choices.

I looked through the book, studied my list, and made a plan.

"It is very nice of you to help Emily," said Daddy. "I will be happy to buy the things you need to make her costume."

"That is right," said Elizabeth. "Just let us know how we can help you."

I made a list for Daddy and Elizabeth. I felt very important sending them out on a shopping trip with my instructions.

They left after dinner and came back with

everything I needed. I got right to work. But I did not work for very long. Daddy said it was time to go to sleep.

"You need your rest. You can work on the costume tomorrow," he said.

Tomorrow would be Friday, the day of the class party. And I would miss it. I decided not to think about the party. It would only make me sad.

I thought about Emily's costume instead. You know what? That made me feel pretty good.

19

A Special Prize

When I went downstairs on Friday morning, Nannie was covering a big plate of bat cakes with plastic wrap. A little plate sat beside it.

"Good morning. How do you feel?" asked Nannie.

"I am okay. But I will feel even better if you tell me that little plate of cupcakes is for me."

"It is," replied Nannie. "You can have a cupcake-and-milk snack later."

Just then Daddy came into the kitchen.

"Hi, honey. How do you feel?" he asked.

"Pretty good. In fact, I feel good enough to go to a party. I think I will go upstairs and get dressed."

Daddy smiled. He knew I was joking.

"I am sorry," he said. "But you know you have to stay home awhile longer."

Then Elizabeth walked in. "Hi, Karen. How are you feeling?" she asked.

I thought about going upstairs and making a sign that said, *I am better.* Instead I just said, "Pretty good."

"I am glad," replied Elizabeth. "I will drop off the food for your class party on my way to work. Daddy and I picked up plenty of soda at the store last night."

"You mean witches' brew."

Elizabeth laughed. She took the plate of bat cakes out to the car. When she returned, she was carrying an envelope. My name was written on it in big letters.

"This was under the door," said Elizabeth.

I opened the envelope. It was a card from

Hannie and Nancy. On the front was a picture of a chicken. Inside it said:

We miss you. Feel better soon!
Love,
Hannie Cow   Nancy Sheep

"That is so nice," said Nannie. "Hannie and Nancy are very good friends."

They sure are! Nancy called me as soon as she got home from school that afternoon.

"We won a special prize!" said Nancy. "You and Hannie and I. We each got a sheet of pumpkin stickers. Hannie said she would slip yours under your door."

"How could I win if I was not there?" I asked.

"We drew a picture of you in your chicken costume. We did not tell you in case we did not win anything. But we did win."

"Wow, thanks!" I said. "Hang on a minute. I will be right back."

I ran to the front door. Sure enough, an-

other envelope was waiting. My pumpkin stickers were inside with a note that said, *We won!*

I ran back to the phone.

"I got my stickers! And I got your card this morning. Thanks a lot," I said.

I called Hannie and she told me more about the party. By the time I finished talking to my friends, I felt almost as if I had been there. I was glad my jack-o'-lantern had been there for real. My friends said he was a big hit when he was lit up.

It had turned out to be a pretty good day. I was almost finished making Emily's costume. I had my prize stickers. And I was itching only a little bit.

The weekend might not be so easy, though. The next day was Sam's bake sale. I was going to miss that. And Sunday was Halloween. I was going to miss trick-or-treating. That felt worst of all.

A Happy Halloween

Saturday turned out to be a good day after all. I found out I could go back to school on Tuesday. I finished Emily's costume and she loved it. And Sam held his bake sale and it was a big success.

"Thanks to you, little sister!" he said. "It would not have been half as good without your help. We made record profits this year. That means we can definitely take our class trip for spring break."

"Cool!" I said.

Now I had two things to be gigundoly

proud of. A great costume for Emily and a great bake sale for Sam. I had done my jobs well, even if I was sick.

Then came Sunday. Halloween. My family kept me busy most of the day. We read Halloween stories and played spooky games. I helped Andrew with his skeleton costume. (He was going trick-or-treating with a school friend and her parents.) I made a few small changes on Emily's costume. Finally it was time for trick-or-treating.

"Will you help put Emily's costume on?" asked Nannie.

"Sure," I replied.

Here is what Emily looked like. She was a fuzzy brown goat with brown leggings and a fuzzy brown sweater. I had made her brown-and-white cardboard horns, a brown pipe-cleaner tail, and a snowy-white cotton beard. I hung a bell around her neck from a red collar. She was the cutest goat I had ever seen.

Emily thought so too. She was so excited that she ran around the house making goat noises. Her costume was every bit as good as my chicken costume.

Daddy looked pretty great too. He was wearing farmer overalls. And he was carrying two trick-or-treat bags.

"Emily will carry one bag for herself, and I will carry the other one for you," said Daddy.

"Thank you," I replied.

I felt sad seeing them all dressed up when I could not go. But I did not want to be a meanie-mo.

"Have a good time," I said.

If I had not been sick, Daddy would have gone trick-or-treating with the Three Musketeers. I was sorry Hannie and Nancy would not get to see him dressed as a farmer. I was even sorrier they would not get to see Emily's costume.

It was hard watching Daddy and Emily leave. And it was hard hearing trick-or-treaters ringing the doorbell when I could not go downstairs and see them.

I climbed into bed with my new spooky

joke book. (It was a thank-you present from Sam.) I thought it might cheer me up.

It might have if I had stayed awake. But I fell asleep and did not wake up until I heard Emily call, "Candy, Karen!" She dropped a full trick-or-treat bag on my bed.

"How do you feel?" asked Daddy.

"Not bad," I replied. "I fell asleep."

"We met up with Hannie and Nancy," said Daddy. "They said you should put on your chicken costume even if you cannot go trick-or-treating. I thought that was an excellent idea. I will take pictures of you and Emily."

Elizabeth came in and helped me put on my costume.

"By the way, I heard the Dager kids had chicken pox. You and Emily played with them a couple of weeks ago, didn't you?" said Daddy.

"Yes! That must be where we got them!" I said.

So I did not get sick because of Emily. I did not get sick because Daddy would not let me move out. I definitely did not get sick because Hannie's and Nancy's plans did not work. I got sick just because I got the same germs Emily did.

I had missed trick-or-treating. But I still had a bagful of treats. I was wearing my costume. And Elizabeth was about to take a picture.

"Smile, everyone," she said.

"We should sing 'Old MacDonald,' " said Daddy.

He started singing, "Old MacDonald had a farm!"

Emily and I joined in. Then *snap*! Elizabeth took our picture. E-I-E-I-O!

L. GODWIN

About the Author

ANN M. MARTIN lives in New York City and loves animals, especially cats. She has two cats of her own, Gussie and Woody.

Other books by Ann M. Martin that you might enjoy are *Stage Fright*; *Me and Katie (the Pest)*; and the books in *The Baby-sitters Club* series.

Ann likes ice cream and *I Love Lucy*. And she has her own little sister, whose name is Jane.

Little Sister

Don't miss #115

KAREN'S RUNAWAY TURKEY

Inside, Ms. Kellogg led us down a hallway and into a room that looked like it could be someone's living room. Someone's fancy living room. A big chandelier, made of glass, hung from the ceiling. A huge oriental rug covered the floor. And all around were antique chairs on spindly legs and little tables with marble tops. The furniture looked almost too good to sit on.

"This place looks like a museum," I whispered to Hannie.

"It is a museum," Hannie whispered back.

In the big room, more people congratulated us. Then Ms. Kellogg led us outside again toward the back of the building. "I'm sure you are all eager to see your prize," she said.

We followed Ms. Kellogg toward a small pen covered with chicken wire. Whatever was inside the pen started squawking.

"This is your prize," I heard Ms. Kellogg say. I could not see the prize right away because I was at the back of the line. But I heard Pamela Harding say, "A turkey? We won a turkey?"